Adapted by Alice Alfonsi

Based on the television series, "That's So Raven", created by Michael Poryes and Susan Sherman

Part One is based on the episode written by Michael Carrington

Part Two is based on the episode written by Marc Warren

New York

Printed in the United States of America

First Edition
1 3 5 7 9 10 8 6 4 2

Library of Congress Control Number: 2005904910

ISBN 0-7868-3837-X

For more Disney Press fun, visit www.disneybooks.com
Visit DisneyChannel.com

Part One

Chapter One

"**O**h, no, you *don't*," Raven Baxter muttered, striding down the front hall.

She had just spied her little brother, Cory, coming down the staircase. And she didn't have to be psychic to know where he was heading!

Cory froze in his tracks when he spotted his sister. Then his gaze shifted to the TV remote control on the coffee table. Once again, I face off with my foe, he thought. But am I truly ready to rise to the challenge and claim another victory?

Raven frowned, seeing her brother's wack expression. Nuh-uh! she thought. That little TV-hogging worm is *not* going to win this time!

An instant later, Cory and Raven were leaping into action. Raven took three big steps and threw herself across the couch. Cory thundered down the staircase and lunged for the coffee table.

In one smooth motion, Raven rolled into a sitting position with the remote-control device in her hand. But she hadn't won yet. With a mighty lunge, Cory snagged a piece of it.

"Give me that!" Cory cried, yanking the plastic gadget with all his might.

"No, Cory!" Raven jerked her end back with a mighty tug. "*Video Countdown* is on." Her favorite TV show was broadcast just once a week—on Saturday morning. And she was *not* going to miss it again!

"No, Raven," Cory whined, pulling the remote his way again. "I'm watching the Cash Channel!" *Stock Market Recap* was about to start, and he needed to check his investments!

"Videos!" Raven insisted, pulling back.

"Cash!" Cory cried.

"Videos!"

"Cash!"

With a final burst of strength, Raven won the tug-of-war. "Ah-hah!" she yelled, raising the remote control high.

Grinning triumphantly, she turned on the TV and flipped the channel. *Video Countdown* was opening its show with one of the hottest songs on the charts, "Kickin' It 4 U." The slammin' hip-hop number boomed through the television's speakers.

"Whoa, that's my jam!" Raven exclaimed. She jumped to her feet and started moving to the beat, thinking, This song has got it goin' on!

Cory rolled his eyes. There goes my stupid sister again, he thought. By now that tune must be sealed in her brain—what little there is of it!

Just then, Mr. and Mrs. Baxter came down the staircase. Mr. Baxter was lugging two heavy suitcases in his meaty fists. Mrs. Baxter had her big purse and an overnight bag slung over her shoulder.

After setting down their bags near the front door, Raven's parents watched their daughter bustin' moves around the living room. They waited for her to stop, but she was totally oblivious.

At last, Mrs. Baxter walked up to her daughter. "Raven," she called. "Raven!"

But Raven wasn't listening. Her eyes were closed, and she was still getting jiggy with her all-time favorite jam.

Frustrated, Raven's father walked into the room, seized the remote, and switched off the television. The music stopped, but Raven didn't. She was still getting down with the beat in her head.

Mrs. Baxter cleared her throat, and Raven finally looked up. "Hey, Mom. That's my jam!" she exclaimed, wiggling and shaking. Then she caught her mother's frown. "Uh—and I can stop any time I want," Raven quickly added.

But Rae's booty was still moving. Finally, she reached back and grabbed it. "Stop!" she commanded. At last, all jiggying ceased.

"Raven," Mr. Baxter said in a stern voice, "this is very important."

Raven nodded, all ears.

"We're going away this weekend," he reminded her, "overnight to cousin Brenda's wedding. And we want to feel comfortable that we're leaving the house with somebody responsible."

Raven nodded. She'd heard this before, of course, about a thousand times! "All right!" she replied. "You can trust me."

But her parents didn't look very convinced.

They exchanged wary glances before picking up their suitcases and heading for the door.

When Raven saw their expressions, she knew she should reassure them. There was no need to worry. Not with Raven Baxter in the house!

"I promise. You can count on me," she told them, crossing her heart.

With a quick nod, Mr. and Mrs. Baxter continued out the door. They had a long drive ahead of them, and they were already running late.

Raven waved good-bye. She was about to close the door behind them, when her father suddenly turned around. "Oh!" he said, poking his head back inside. "We left you a turkey in the refrigerator."

Raven nodded. "Got it!" She tried to close the door again, but this time her mother turned back.

"Oh, and remember," Mrs. Baxter said, "Reverend Mattson is coming by tomorrow to give you your letter of recommendation."

"Got it!" Raven chirped again.

But her mom *still* looked worried. With a sigh, Raven leaned close and squeezed her mother's shoulder. "Look," she said sincerely, "I will not mess this up, okay? That letter is going to get me my internship in fashion design."

Mrs. Baxter smiled, relief finally relaxing her tense expression. "Good-bye, honey," she said, kissing her daughter.

"All right, so don't worry," Raven sang out with a grin. "You guys have a great trip, okay? Buh-bye!"

Finally, Raven closed the front door behind her parents and bolted the lock. "Phew!" she said, facing Cory. "I thought they'd never leave!"

Her little brother rolled his big brown eyes. "Tell me about it," he said. Then he ran to the window and pushed the curtain aside. Cory patiently watched his parents load the car and drive away. When he was absolutely sure they were gone, he strode to the couch and plopped down. Leaning forward, he felt around underneath the coffee table.

Raven folded her arms and eyed her brother with suspicion. "Cory, what are you doing?"

Cory smiled as his fingers found the square edges of a manila envelope. He'd taped it under the coffee table a long time ago. *Rip!* With one sharp tug, he pulled the envelope free of its hiding place.

Curious, Raven walked over to the couch and dropped down next to her brother.

"Bam!" said Cory, dropping the envelope in her lap.

Uh-oh, Raven thought. Cory's more excited

about this envelope than I was about the TV remote. And since "Evil Little Plotter" is the worm's favorite Internet screen name, whatever's in his envelope *cannot* be good.

"Okay, Cory, what's in there?" Raven asked as she picked it up. Four words were scrawled in large, crude letters on the outside. "'In case parents leave'?" she read aloud.

A devilish grin crossed Cory's face. "Oh, I've been planning for this day for a *long* time."

Now, Raven truly was worried. She tore open the envelope and leafed through its contents. "Tickets? A guest list?" she said, pawing through the small stack of stuff. "Cory, what is all this for?"

"For the party that we're throwing tonight," he replied.

Raven shook her head. "Oh, no, no." She stuffed the papers back into the envelope. "We are *not* going to be throwing a party, okay. Because if we mess this up, Mom and Dad will *never . . . trust us . . . again*!"

Cory shrugged. "I'm *assuming* we're going to mess up. That's why we might as well throw a party and go out with a bang!"

Raven was tempted. She truly was. But she'd just promised her parents they could trust her! "Forget it, all right," she told her brother sternly. "I'm the boss, and I say no."

Dang, she thought with a freaked-out shudder. I'm starting to sound like Dad!

Cory didn't say anything for a few seconds. Finally, his shoulders slumped. "You're right," he said. "I'm sorry. Forget I even brought that up."

Raven sighed with relief. "Very good," she said, and patted her brother's head as if he were an obedient puppy. "Good Cory," she cooed.

Oh, snap! Raven thought with another shudder. Now I'm sounding like Mom!

With a sigh, Raven headed to the kitchen with Cory's envelope. She didn't know whether her brother was being serious or just playing her. But she wasn't going to take any chances. She still had his envelope of plans, and she had a plan, too—to toss it into the trash can.

Cory waited until his sister left. When he was sure that he was alone, he crossed the living room and sat down at the piano. But he wasn't there to practice his scales.

With one hand, he reached down and felt around underneath the baby grand. When his fingers touched the edge of an envelope, he smiled.

"Oh, yeah!" he whispered, pulling the envelope free. *Rip!*

He now held a second manila envelope that

looked just like the first. Across its surface was scrawled in big, bold letters:

IN CASE RAVEN SAYS NO

"Bam!" Cory cried. Then he busted some moves to his own private song—*It's party time!*

Chapter Two

Later that day, Raven came down the back stairs to find Cory doing housework. He held a paper towel in one hand and a bottle of cleanser in the other. And he was actually wiping down the kitchen counters.

Raven blinked in something close to shock. "You're cleaning?"

Cory nodded. "Mom and Dad are away, and you need the house to be spotless when Reverend Mattson comes over tomorrow."

Raven's shock turned into uneasy suspicion. "This is not like you," she said.

Cory did his very best to appear wounded. "Raven," he said, putting a hand over his heart, "a person can change."

"A person, yes," she replied. "*You* . . . I don't know so much."

Cory shrugged and turned away. He made it look like he had gone back to cleaning, but he was really checking his watch. Almost time! he thought.

Less than a minute later, loud music pulsed down the back stairs.

"Hey! My jam!" Raven cried, hearing her all-time favorite song again, "Kickin' It 4 U." She threw up her arms and began to shake it!

Cory made a show of slapping his forehead. "I . . . I must have accidentally set my alarm!" he cried, doing his best to sound surprised. "Let me turn it off."

But as Cory moved toward the steps, Raven grabbed his collar. "Don't you go turn that off," she warned. "'Cause you know, that's my jam." Then she turned Cory around to face the kitchen again.

"I'll go turn it *up!*" she said. And, moving her hips to the beat, she danced up the stairs.

Cory grinned in triumph. "Yeah, there *you* go!" he crowed. Once again, he checked his wristwatch. Then he glanced out the kitchen door. Like clockwork, he noticed two figures approaching the back of the house.

"And here *they* come," said Cory. Grinning, he opened the back door. Eddie Thomas and Chelsea Daniels entered.

"Yo, yo, yo, Cory," Eddie said in an urgent whisper. "We got your message. What's the big secret?"

"Yeah. And why did we have to be here at exactly ten o'clock?" Chelsea asked.

Upstairs, Raven's song suddenly got louder. Cory knew his sister was pumping up the volume—just as he'd expected!

"Listen," Cory told Raven's best friends. "My parents are away, and we're throwing this giant party."

Chelsea hopped up and down and clapped her hands.

"Eddie, you're going to be the DJ," Cory declared.

Eddie grinned and gave Cory a high five. "I'm all over it."

"And Chelsea, I'm going to need you to pick up some stuff," Cory commanded.

"Okay, sure," Chelsea replied.

Cory pulled two bills out of his pocket. One at a time, he handed them to Chelsea. "Here's twenty bucks for snacks. And here's twenty bucks for decorations."

Chelsea held up the money, one bill in each hand. Suddenly, a look of total distress crossed her face.

"What's wrong?" Cory asked.

"*Man!*" she groaned. "I'm never going to remember which is which!"

"Huh?" said Cory. He stared at Raven's best friend. Chelsea has officially lost it, he thought.

"Hold on," Eddie interrupted. "Are you sure that Rae's gonna be okay with this?"

Cory was ready for that question. "Let's just say she's going to want this party more than any of us," he replied with a smirk.

Upstairs, "Kickin' It 4 U" stopped kicking. The song had ended, and Raven had just turned off Cory's radio alarm.

Don't panic, Cory told himself. You have at least thirty seconds. "Okay! This conversation is over," he cried, pushing Eddie and Chelsea out the back door. "Move, move, move!"

Cory slammed the kitchen door. He grabbed his cleaning stuff and began to polish the sink. Raven skipped down the stairs a moment later. As she passed the back door, she noticed two familiar figures striding away from the house.

"Was that Eddie and Chelsea?" Raven asked.

Cory nodded, his face serious. "Yes," he replied. "And don't worry. I told them that responsible kids aren't allowed to have visitors while their parents are away."

"Very good," said Raven. Then she blinked and scratched her head. "A little *too* good."

All of a sudden, Raven felt a familiar electric tingle shoot through her entire body. The world went in and out of focus, and her mind took a little trip. . . .

**Through her eye
The vision runs
Flash of future
Here it comes—**

Okay, what am I looking at? Oh, it's only the living room and my scheming little worm of a brother, Cory! Already I'm not impressed with this vision.

But wait . . .

Look at the freaked-out expression on Cory's face. He's acting like he's seeing something really scary. Like maybe a blood-sucking monster! Or a horrific-looking alien creature!

He's backing away like he sees a beast so horrible that—hold the phone! His mouth's opening. He's saying something—

"No, Raven, no, no!"

Raven stumbled as she came out of her vision. She reached out and gripped the counter to regain her balance. Cory stood in front of her, paper towel in one hand, cleanser in the other.

"Cory, I just had a vision that I was coming

after you," Raven confided. And, *dang*, she was *not* happy to see her brother looking at her like she was some kind of total beast!

Raven's eyes narrowed with extreme suspicion. "Why, Cory?" she asked. "Why was I coming after you?"

Doing his very best clueless act, Cory just shrugged. "Hey, *you're* the psychic. You tell me."

Raven opened her mouth to speak, but nothing came out. Sometimes she had a hunch about what her visions meant. But this time, she was totally stumped. And Cory was refusing to help.

With a flourish, he picked up the dust mop and furniture wax. "Now, if you'll excuse me, I have responsibilities," Cory briskly snapped. Then he hurried into the living room.

As Raven watched her brother go, her mind began to race through the twisted schemes from Cory's past. Which one, she wondered, is he going to spring on me before Mom and Dad get back? I wish I knew!

Okay, Raven thought, trying to stop being paranoid. I'm not sure what my brother is up to . . . *yet*. But he better understand that he's not going to get away with anything shady this weekend. Not while I'm in the house!

Behind the wheel of the family car, Raven's father sighed and fanned himself. Even with the air conditioner running full blast, the inside of the vehicle was hot. Through closed windows, horns blared and the roar of engines battered his ears.

Raven's mother shook her head as she stared through the windshield at the stalled cars around them. "This traffic is terrible," she proclaimed. "I'm going to get the map and see if there's another way."

Mr. Baxter shook his head. "Uh-uh," he said. "That's why I installed this navigational system." He tapped a small computer mounted to the middle of his dashboard. "I even programmed it to respond to my voice."

A map of the San Francisco region appeared on the computer's small screen. Mrs. Baxter watched her husband flick a switch. Then he actually spoke to the machine.

"Find alternate route, please," Mr. Baxter said loudly.

"Hello, Victor," the computer purred in a feminine voice.

Mrs. Baxter blinked in surprise. "It knows your name?"

"Mmm-hmm," Mr. Baxter replied with obvious pride. "I programmed that, too."

Mrs. Baxter crossed her arms and looked away. Since when are computers so *friendly?* she wondered. And so *female?*

"What else does it know?" she snapped.

"Calculating an alternate route for Victor," the computer's voice cooed.

Mr. Baxter chuckled. "She's calculating for me, Tanya."

Mrs. Baxter turned her head to face her husband. "I know how to read a map, too, you know," she said.

But before Mr. Baxter could reply, the computer spoke again. "Take the next exit and turn right, Victor."

Mrs. Baxter examined the new route displayed on the computer screen. "Old Mill Road!" she exclaimed. "That's going to take us way up into the hills." She stubbornly shook her head. "I don't think so."

Mr. Baxter exhaled in exasperation. "But, Tanya," he said, "she's a highly sophisticated computer system that's tracking us by satellite." He patted the computer with obvious affection. "She knows what she's doing."

Mrs. Baxter folded her arms and glared at the highway ahead. "She'd better."

Chapter Three

To Raven, Cory's whole Mr. Clean act was completely freakish. When she entered the living room, she found him dusting the furniture, the lamps—even under the lampshades!

My brother has got to be playing me, she thought. But until I figure out how and why, I'm just going to let him whistle while he works. For one thing, Mom and Dad will sure appreciate coming home to a really tidy house!

Raven headed for the sofa. She figured she could keep one eye on Cory while checking out the Style Network's runway news. But before she even made it to the couch cushions, Cory hit a button on the stereo's remote control. The throbbing beat of "Kickin' It 4 U" began to shake the room. And Raven began to shake her booty!

"*Whoa!* My jam!" Raven shrieked excitedly. Unable to stop herself, she threw up her arms and swung her hips. "I never get tired of this song," she proclaimed.

Cory quietly snickered. "I know."

While Raven became a dancing fool, Cory dropped his dust mop and sat down on the couch. He dug between the cushions and found the thin strand of fishing wire he'd hid earlier. The nearly invisible wire reached across the room. Its other end was tied to a tall floor lamp. The lamp appeared to be an antique. It had a cast-iron base topped by a multicolored Tiffany-style glass shade.

Cory slowly pulled on the fishing line. The lamp inched out of its corner and across the hardwood floor. While Raven continued kickin' it, Cory tugged on the wire until the lamp stood directly behind her wiggling body.

Lost in the beat, Raven kept on dancing, coming closer and closer to hitting the lamp. But she kept on missing it. Cory couldn't stand it much longer. Gritting his teeth in frustration, he decided to close this deal himself.

"Go, Raven. Go, Raven," Cory chanted, egging her on. He jumped to his feet and clapped his hands. "Now, back, back, back it up!"

Raven nodded happily. Stepping with her brother, she boldly started dancing backward—until her backside struck the lamp and sent it toppling to the floor.

Crash!

Cory covered his mouth in mock surprise. "No, you didn't!" he exclaimed.

"*Oh, snap!*" Raven cried. She turned and stared in horror. The beautiful glass shade had shattered into a hundred pieces on the hardwood floor.

Cory shook his head. "I guess you backed it up *too* far."

"This is Mom's favorite lamp!" Raven wailed. "It was a wedding present from Grandma!"

"But it was an accident," Cory insisted.

Raven didn't care. She knew her mother would be furious—and devastated. She felt positively sick! Putting a hand over her mouth, she began to pace back and forth.

"Raven, it'll be okay," Cory quickly told her.

Raven shook her head. She didn't see how!

"You can replace the lamp before Mom and Dad get home!" Cory assured her. "Problem solved."

Raven slowed her frantic pacing and pondered her brother's words. Could it work? she wondered. Yeah, sure it would! Why not?

"You know what? You're *right*!" Raven told her brother. "I mean, how much could it be?"

Raven followed Cory into the kitchen. Together, they fired up their mom's laptop computer. Once they were online, Cory went to his mother's favorite Web site, Antiques 'R' Us.

"Look!" Raven said. "There's a lamp just like it!"

Cory nodded. "That's the one. I'll just pull it up and find out how much it—"

Suddenly, Cory was speechless.

"How much?!" Raven gasped.

"Wow," Cory whistled, "those antique lamps are *expensive*!"

He glanced up at his sister. Raven was still gawking at the price on the screen. Her jaw had gone slack.

"So, where are you going to get the money

to pay for the lamp?" Cory asked.

Raven sighed. She knew there was only one friend she could go to for this kind of cash. Unfortunately, getting the money out of him was going to take a little hammering.

Ten minutes later, Raven was sitting on the floor in her room. Clutching her beloved pink piggy bank in her arms, she hung her head. It was time to deliver the bad news.

"Well, Mr. Pigsley," Raven whispered, "I've given to you faithfully over the years, and now . . . it's time to give it *back*."

She put the ceramic pig on the floor in front of her and raised the hammer. But when she looked into Mr. Pigsley's big blue eyes, her heart melted. I can't do it. I just can't!

Then Raven thought about her mother coming home and seeing that smashed antique lamp. Oh, snap. I guess I can!

She turned her beloved Mr. Pigsley to face away from her—so he wouldn't see what was coming. "Hey, look," she told her old friend, "that little piggy is going to the market." Then she raised the hammer high. "And you're going all the way home!"

Raven brought the hammer down, and Mr. Pigsley exploded. Broken pottery pieces and change scattered across her bedroom floor.

"Okay, let's see what we've got," Raven said. With the edge of the heavy hammer, she pushed the pottery shards out of the way. Then she eyeballed the coins. Right away, she could see she was in big trouble.

"This is it?" she wailed.

Just then, Cory entered the room. He saw Raven's life savings spilled out on the floor. "Got enough for the lamp?" he asked.

Raven shook her head. "No. I don't even have enough for the *bulb*."

Cory wasn't surprised in the least. The pathetic handful of change from Raven's piggy bank wouldn't buy squat, and Cory had figured on that all along.

As the only miser in the Baxter family, Cory had been stockpiling loot for years—birthday money, holiday cash, coins recovered from sofa cushions. But the real key to Cory's small fortune was investing. He'd learned how to make his money work for him.

When will my sister ever learn? he thought. You can't get compound interest from pottery!

Raven stood up and faced her brother. Mr. Pigsley's assassination hammer was still clutched tightly in her hand. "Cory," she said, desperation in her eyes, "can I borrow some money?"

Eyeing the hammer, Cory took a fearful step backward. "Put the hammer down, and we can talk about it."

Raven rolled her eyes. She dropped the tool on her desk, then faced her brother expectantly.

"Sorry," Cory replied. "I wish I could help, but my money's all tied up."

Raven's eyes narrowed with skepticism. "In what?" she demanded.

Cory shrugged. "A little of this, a little of that," he said. "I'm *diversified*."

Raven frowned and her eyes misted. "But what am I going to do?"

Cory paced the room, pretending to ponder Raven's question. Finally, he snapped his fingers and whirled to face her. "Wait a second!" he cried. "What was that *thing* I wanted to do while Mom and Dad were away?"

"Have a party?" Raven said with a defeated sigh.

Cory nodded his head enthusiastically. "Maybe charge admission," he suggested.

Raven didn't like it—not one bit! The whole thing just sounded wrong. She'd be crazy-stupid to agree to anything her little rat brother suggested. But . . . she was really stuck. What choice did she have?

"Okay, well," Raven said, "let's say we *do* throw a party, there have to be rules, Cory."

Cory nodded, his head wobbling up and down like a bobble-head doll.

"All right," Raven continued, trying to think things through. She had to get this right with Cory now, or it all could go totally wrong.

"When we have this party," Raven declared, "the people who come have to be quiet, well-behaved, and *totally* under control."

Chapter Four

"**T**his party is totally out of control!" Raven cried that evening.

Unfortunately, in the middle of all the noise and dancing bodies, nobody heard her. Eddie was certainly too busy to notice. He was playing tracks at a temporary DJ stand. Eyes closed, headphones on, he was totally caught up in the remix beat.

Cory couldn't hear Raven, either. He was too busy collecting "contributions" from the throng of kids lining up at the front door. There were so many people that Raven could hardly move. But that was no surprise—not when Raven's house displayed a great big sign out front that proclaimed PARTY HERE!

Music poured through the open windows and doors. The throbbing hip-hop rocked the entire neighborhood. The noise level was something less than an atom bomb's, but not much.

Colorful balloons filled the corners and hung from the ceiling. Dozens of beach balls rolled around on the floor or sailed across the room as kids tossed and kicked them.

Raven stood in the center of the chaos, wringing her hands as teens continued to flow into the house. "Please get down off there! Stop dancing on the couch!" she yelled at a boy and girl.

It was a nonstop job keeping the dancers off the furniture and the noise level below earth-shattering. Somebody had to do it. Raven knew her brother Cory wasn't going to bother. He was too busy at the front door.

"Come on in," Cory said to a new girl. He smiled warmly, welcoming her. But before she could get more than two feet beyond the front door, he thrust his palm under her chin and added, "That'll be five bucks!"

After the girl handed over a five-dollar bill, Cory greeted the next person the same way. And the next, and the next. "Come on in. That'll be five bucks. Come on in. That'll be five bucks. Come on in. . . ."

At least Cory was raking in the cash, Raven told herself. Replacing her mom's favorite lamp wouldn't be cheap. She only hoped there'd be enough left over to save the *rest* of the house from total destruction!

Darting her way through the crowd, Raven headed for the DJ stand. "Eddie, this party is way out of hand," she yelled over the noise of the crowd.

Eddie grinned. "And pretty soon it's gonna

be way off the hook!" he cried. Then he leaned into the microphone and shouted, "Everybody jump!"

And everyone did. The huge crowd went up and came down. Their landing shook the house—and possibly the neighborhood. If Eddie does that again, Raven thought, my neighbors are going to think we're having an earthquake!

Meanwhile, on the other side of the room, the Baxter phone rang. Chelsea was standing nearby, so she picked it up.

"Hello?" she said.

"Hello. This is Reverend Mattson," the caller began.

Because of all the party noise, Chelsea could hardly understand the man. "Reggie Madison?" she said.

"I was supposed to come over tomorrow," Reverend Mattson continued. "But I'll be in the neighborhood, so I thought I'd stop by tonight."

Chelsea understood that part of the conversation and nodded enthusiastically. "Okay, sure. Come on over, Reggie."

Chelsea hung up before Raven could reach her. Finally, Raven pushed through the mob and asked Chelsea, "Hey, hey. Who was that?"

Chelsea shrugged. "I don't know. But he sounded kind of cute!"

Raven watched her friend wander away. Well, she thought, at least it wasn't Mom or Dad checking up on us. So far, our secret is safe.

"Hey, look! It's Matthew!" someone called.

Raven looked up. She didn't know this cute guy named Matthew very well, but he'd obviously turned into the life of the party—the *out-of-control* party. He walked past Raven wearing a bathing suit, snorkel, swim fins, and a bright yellow flotation tube around his waist.

"Hey, everybody into the pool!" Matthew announced. Then he ran up the stairs. A bunch of kids cheered and followed.

"Wait a second," Raven cried. "We don't have a pool!" And even if we did, she realized, it would *not* be on the second floor!

While Raven was being driven to distraction, her parents were just plain driving . . . and driving and driving!

For two hours, Mr. and Mrs. Baxter had been traveling along Old Mill Road. The sun had set long ago, and the rural route was dark and deserted.

Finally, a pleasant female voice broke the silence inside the car. "Continue on present road for five-point-three miles, Victor."

Raven's father nodded obediently at the voice of his computer navigational system. "I sure will," he replied. "Five-point-three wide-open, traffic-free miles. Thanks."

"Anything for you, Victor," the electronic voice cooed.

Raven's mother frowned at the bright little screen affixed to the dashboard. "Anything for you, Victor," she snapped.

Mr. Baxter threw his wife a defensive look. "What?" he said. "I got the polite model."

Mrs. Baxter crossed her arms angrily. "Well, your polite little friend here has us on a dirt road in the middle of nowhere!"

"Tanya, relax," Mr. Baxter said. "This is a shortcut. We'll be there in exactly five-point-three—"

Just then, Mr. Baxter slammed on the brakes. In the glare of the headlights, he read the sign on the big barrier blocking the road in front of them.

BEWARE! BRIDGE OUT. ROAD CLOSED.

"Road closed?!" Mrs. Baxter cried.

"That's impossible," Mr. Baxter said.

Mrs. Baxter looked at her husband, then at the computer on the dashboard. "Mmm-hmm," she said with attitude.

The electronic voice spoke up. "It appears I've made an error. . . . My bad, Victor."

Mr. Baxter patted the top of the computer screen. "Don't worry about it," he said in a comforting tone. "There's no way you were going to know—"

Mrs. Baxter threw up her hands. "And will you *stop* talking to that thing. We have to get back to the freeway. You realize we're never going to make the wedding now."

Raven's mother pointed a threatening finger at the navigation system. "You are one big waste of money," she declared.

Mr. Baxter frowned. "Tanya, please don't talk to Sasha that way."

Mrs. Baxter's jaw dropped. "You *named* her?"

"Uh . . . no. No, no, no," Mr. Baxter claimed. "See, Sasha stands for . . . uh, uh—"

Mrs. Baxter raised a suspicious eyebrow and waited.

"It means, it means . . ." Tightly gripping the steering wheel, Mr. Baxter thought it over for a few seconds. "Safe . . . Arrival . . . System . . . Helping . . . Americans," he said. On the last word, Raven's father finally relaxed and leaned back.

Mrs. Baxter rolled her eyes. "Come on, Victor! You just made that up. I can't believe you are in love with a stupid gadget."

"That's ridiculous," Mr. Baxter declared. "And don't call Sasha stupid!"

"Okay, listen up," Mrs. Baxter commanded. "Get us back to the freeway, pronto!"

Mr. Baxter shook his head. "I told you. Sasha only responds to *my* voice."

Mrs. Baxter's eyes narrowed. "I was talking to *you*, Victor!"

Chapter Five

Tink! Tink! Tinkka tink . . . Tink! Tink! Tinkka tink! The sound of clanging metal was coming out of the kitchen. It grated on Raven's nerves, and she burst through the door to put a stop to the awful racket.

She found Matthew the party animal with a spoon in his hand, banging a pot. His shirt was still off from his no-pool swim, and his spandex-covered rear was parked in the middle of her dad's countertop.

Tink! Tink! Tinkka tink . . . Tink! Tink! Tinkka tink!

"Hey!" Raven shouted. "What kind of game is that?! That's my dad's good pot! Get off the counter," she commanded Matthew.

A moment later, Cory and Eddie burst into the kitchen. Raven collared her little brother. "Cory, haven't we made enough money to pay for that lamp yet?"

Cory shook his head. "Nope. Not even close. Besides, we've got bigger problems."

"Yeah," Eddie cried. "There's a lot of hungry people around here and no food." Eddie opened the refrigerator and checked the contents. "Hey, Rae, okay if I put this out?" he asked, grabbing a platter with a big baked turkey.

"Eddie, I don't know," Raven said. "My dad made that for me and Cory."

But before Eddie could slip the bird back into the fridge, a crowd of hungry kids swarmed him. "Yo, yo, yo, take it easy!" he cried.

Within seconds, there was nothing left but a carcass. When the kids finally left, Eddie counted on his hands, then sighed in relief. "At least I've still got all my fingers!"

Just then, Chelsea poked her head through the kitchen door. "Cory, did you order a mechanical—"

"Yes!" whooped Cory. "Now we can get this party started!"

"A mechanical what?" Raven cried. "Cory, tell me! A mechanical what?" But her brother had already raced into the living room.

All right, she thought, this party is officially over the top. And it's time to put an end to it. Raven faced the kids still hanging in the kitchen.

"People, people!" Raven called, clapping her hands. Everyone looked up. "Hello," Raven said politely. "I want to thank you all for coming. Now I want to thank you all for *leaving*. So if you would exit the rear door and—"

Raven's speech came to an abrupt halt when

she opened the kitchen door. Reverend Mattson was standing outside, poised in midknock.

"Hello," Raven gulped. Then she slammed the door and turned around. "Okay," she told the kids in the kitchen, "party in the living room!"

But no one moved.

All right, think! Raven told herself. How do you move a room full of hungry kids out of a kitchen? I've got it! She rushed to the refrigerator and searched it for something large enough to feed the crowd. A two-foot-long salami was all she could find.

"Salami break," she yelled, tossing the tube of meat into the living room.

The kids stampeded after it. Then Raven hurried to the back door and opened it again. Reverend Mattson was still standing there. Behind his large glasses, he blinked in confusion.

"Hello, Reverend Mattson," Raven said brightly, turning on the charm. "Sorry about the door. We've just got to get that spring fixed!"

Reverend Mattson accepted her apology with a smile. "I was in the neighborhood, so I thought I'd drop by, with *jubilation*, to give you your letter of *recommendation*."

"Right, and I thank you with much . . . *appreciation*," said Raven. "And I know you've got to get back to your *congregation*."

She reached for the letter, but the reverend pulled it away. Oh, snap! she thought. This had better not take too long. She needed that letter to secure her spot in the fashion intern program. And there was no way he'd give it to her if he saw what was going on in the next room.

She silently thanked her lucky stars that the reverend had approached the house from the back and not the front. That PARTY HERE! sign would have been a little hard to miss!

"It was such a pleasure to write about a young woman of such fine character and strong moral values," the reverend said.

Just then, Raven heard "Kickin' It 4 U" begin to play in the next room. That's my jam, Raven realized. Desperately, she fought the jiggy urge. No, stop, she silently begged her wiggling hips. *Stop!*

Reverend Mattson looked at her strangely. "Are you okay?" he asked.

Raven nodded, finding it almost impossible not to bob her head to the beat. "Yes. And thank you for asking. I'll just take that letter."

Raven reached for it again. But Reverend Mattson yanked it back once more. "You know, that music is awfully loud," he noted.

"You know what? That's actually from next

door, really." Raven shook her head in mock disapproval. "Those party animals."

The reverend gave Raven a surprised look. "Grandma Butterfield? Why, she just had her hip replaced."

"Well, then she must be hip-hoppin'!" Raven replied. Taking the reverend's arm, she tried to encourage him to leave. "Thanks for coming, buh-bye."

All of a sudden, Matthew burst into the kitchen from the living room. The crazy kid still had his shirt off. Someone had painted the word "party" on his chest in big gold letters.

Oh, no, no, no! Raven thought, I cannot let the reverend see this guy! In desperation, she grabbed the first thing she could reach—a can of cheese spread next to a plate of crackers on the kitchen table.

"Oh, hey, Reverend Mattson. Would you like some cheese and crackers?" Raven raised the can high, hit the nozzle, and sprayed gooey yellow cheese all over the preacher's glasses.

Blinded, Reverend Mattson reached out his arms like a zombie. Raven hustled Matthew back to the living room before the kid could say something stupid.

"Raven, what in the world?" said Reverend Mattson. He took off his glasses and set them on the counter.

"Uh, you know what? Faulty nozzle," Raven said. "You put cheese in a can, you're just asking for trouble. Am I right?"

Raven grabbed the reverend's arm and forcefully ushered him to the door. "I know you have to be going, okay, so if you would please just exit this way, and give me that—" Raven snatched the letter out of Reverend Mattson's hand.

"Yes," the reverend said. "Well, good luck with your internship."

"And good luck with your flock," Raven replied. "Okay, buh-bye!"

Raven slammed the back door. She hardly had time for a breath when the sound of cheers and whooping erupted in the living room.

"What now?" Raven groaned. She stumbled through the kitchen door and nearly screamed. In the center of the living room, Eddie was riding an immense mechanical bull. The crowd of kids was cheering him on!

Raven freaked and grabbed her brother's arm. "Cory, a mechanical bull!" she cried. "What were you thinking?!"

Cory lifted the bucket of money in his hand. "I was thinking two dollars a ride!"

"Yee-holla!" Eddie cried as he spun on the bull. Finally, the machine slowed to a halt and Eddie dismounted. He stumbled for a moment, disoriented, then saw Raven. "That was so fun, Rae. I want to do it again," he cried. Then he collapsed into a dizzy heap.

"All right, Cory, I'm next!" Chelsea dropped two bills into Cory's bucket and climbed into the saddle.

"You're going to ride the bull?" Cory asked in surprise.

"Sure," Chelsea replied. "I rode one at a vegetarian dude ranch. Except it wasn't a bull. It was a cabbage."

While Chelsea climbed into the leather saddle, Raven turned to her brother. "Okay, so you do realize that the reverend was just here," she informed him.

Cory shrugged. "Well, did you get your letter?" he asked.

"Yes, I did," Raven replied.

"And we earned enough money to pay for the lamp," Cory told her.

Raven blinked in surprise. "We did?"

"Yeah," said Cory. "So *relax*."

"Yeah, Rae," Eddie said, putting an arm around her. "Have some fun. Join the party."

Slowly, Raven nodded her head. "Yeah, you're right," she decided at last. "I might as well enjoy it."

Chelsea certainly was. From the back of the bucking mechanical bull, she let out a loud cowgirl whoop. "Well, it's no cabbage," she called to Cory, "but it's still fun!"

Chapter Six

On an empty, dark road in the middle of nowhere, Raven's father was still driving. He tried not to look at the dashboard. The blank screen and dangling wires of his brand-new navigational system were just too painful to see.

"You didn't have to unplug her," he muttered to his wife.

"You didn't have to name her!" Mrs. Baxter replied.

Mr. Baxter thought it over and sighed. "I guess I did get a little attached," he confessed.

Now Mrs. Baxter sighed. "Maybe I did get a little jealous," she admitted.

Mr. Baxter checked his watch. "Well," he

said, "looks like we're never going to make it to the wedding. What do you want to do?"

Mrs. Baxter hated to give up on the trip, but there was no reason to keep driving. "I guess we should just head home," she said. "I hope Sasha can get us back to the freeway."

Mr. Baxter smiled when he saw his wife plugging the navigational system back in. We may be lost, he thought. But all may not be lost!

"You know what," Mr. Baxter told his wife, "I did see a sign for a little country inn. Maybe we could have our own little vacation without the kids."

"Ooh," Mrs. Baxter exclaimed with delight. "Mama like!"

"Raven?" Reverend Mattson called from the Baxters' back door. "I seem to have forgotten my glasses."

The reverend didn't see Raven in the kitchen, so he let himself in. He glanced around the room and quickly spotted his glasses on the counter. They were still covered with cheese, so he reached for a paper towel and started to clean them.

The music he'd heard earlier was louder than ever now. And another sound caught his attention. Voices—*a lot* of them—were chanting Raven's name.

"Raven! Raven! Raven! Raven . . ."

My goodness, the reverend thought. All those voices sound as if they're right in the next room!

Curious, the reverend put his cheese-free glasses back on and followed the noise to the living room.

Raven was having the time of her life. This mechanical bull is the bomb, she thought.

She held the saddle horn with one hand and threw the other high overhead—just like a rodeo star.

Eddie was in the corner playing his slammin' tracks, and all the kids were chanting Raven's name.

"Raven! Raven! Raven! Raven . . ."

"Wheeeeeehaaaaaa!" Raven squealed with joy, until she heard her name again—

"Raven!"

But this voice wasn't like the others. It was deep and stern and not very happy. Raven turned her head toward the kitchen door and confirmed what she dreaded.

"Reverend!" she cried. Her eyes bugged out, and her grin turned into a grimace.

Reverend! The crowd of kids heard Raven, and they turned to see the preacher now standing in their presence. Since Reverend Mattson knew almost every one of their parents, all the cheering and stomping and partying came to a screeching halt.

Frantically, Raven searched her mind for some sort of explanation. "How did this bull get in here?" she cried. "And how did I get on it? Cory, turn this off!"

Flustered, Cory misunderstood. "Turn it up?"

Before Raven could correct him, her little brother had dialed the mechanical bull up to its highest speed. The bull started to buck wildly. And Raven found herself holding on for dear life.

"Turn it off!" she shrieked. "*Off!*"

Cory cringed, realizing his mistake. "Sorry, my bad!" he called and snapped off the power. The bull stopped too fast and Raven went flying. She sailed over the heads of the crowd and landed right in front of the reverend.

Quickly, Raven scrambled to her feet and

adjusted her clothes. "How y'all doin', Reverend?" she asked cheerfully.

The reverend's voice was stern. "Raven, what's going on here?"

Raven tried not to panic. Okay, Rae, she told herself, make it good! "Um, this is my, uh, study group," she said, gesturing to the freaked-out crowd, standing around the mechanical bull. Taking Raven's cue, the paralyzed kids nodded in unison.

"Yeah!" Raven continued. "And we were just at the part where they started to discuss . . ."

Think! Raven told herself. And remember that you're talking to a preacher, so make it good!

"Uh . . . he who rideth longeth on the bullith," she cried, waving a righteous finger in the air, "shall receive . . . forgivenesseth."

The reverend glanced up at the kids packing the room. Everyone quickly bowed their heads. It didn't help. "Looks to me like you were having a party while your parents are away," the reverend said evenly.

Raven gulped. "Yeah, um, see, now I can see how you could get that impression, Reverend. But if you take away the music, the people, and the mechanical bull, it's all very innocent."

"Yo, check it out!" cried Matthew. He abruptly appeared at the top of the stairs. "We just put twelve kids in your bathtub! That's a new record!"

Raven cringed. That crazy party animal had failed to notice the reverend's arrival. Great, she thought, now what's the reverend going to say?

Reverend Mattson's reply was just one word. "Matthew?"

At the top of the stairs, the party animal blinked. "Dad?"

"Party over!" Eddie cried.

All the kids agreed. In one great swarm, they lunged for the door.

"Great party, Rae!" Chelsea cried, rushing into the night. "See ya Sunday, Reggie!"

The reverend frowned. "I'll see you *all* Sunday," he called after them. Spotting his son, he added, "And I'll see *you* at home."

Matthew hung his head and kept moving. Then Reverend Mattson faced the one girl who had nowhere to run. "Raven," he said, "I'm very disappointed in you. *And* . . . I'm going to need that letter back."

Crushed, Raven pulled out the reverend's recommendation letter. "Reverend, I've been waiting for this internship all year," she pleaded.

But the reverend shook his head. "I'm sorry, Raven. But you should have thought about that before you threw this party."

With a sigh of total defeat, Raven handed him the letter. Her eyes misted. I blew the one thing that could really help me achieve my dream, she thought. And the worst part of all was that I *knew* better all along. I never wanted to throw this party in the first place!

The reverend tucked the letter into his jacket. But as he started for the front door, Cory stepped forward.

"Reverend," he called.

"Cory, not now," Raven warned. Things were bad enough. She feared her little brother would only make it worse.

"This is all my fault," Cory confessed.

What! Raven thought. "Continue," she urged.

"My sister shouldn't get any of the blame for this," Cory said. "I made Raven think she broke an expensive lamp, but it was really a cheap imitation. And I was going to put the real lamp back and keep all the money from the party."

Raven was speechless for a moment. Finally,

she said, "You know, Cory, you've done some pretty lowdown things, but this has to be the worst."

Cory hung his head. "I know, I know. I'm sorry. I hope you're not telling Mom and Dad."

Reverend Mattson peered down at Cory with a stern look. "Oh, don't worry, Cory, she won't. 'Cause *you'll* probably want to tell them *yourself.*"

"I will?" Cory squealed. Then he caught sight of the reverend's expression. "I mean, *I will.*"

"And Raven," continued the reverend, "even though you showed some poor judgment, any sister who has a little brother willing to speak up on her behalf must be a pretty good person." He pulled out his letter of recommendation and handed it back to her. "Have fun at your internship," he told her with a smile. "But not *too much* fun."

"Thank you, Reverend," Raven said sincerely. "Thanks, and drive safe!"

After the reverend had gone, Raven wheeled on Cory. "Now it's time to deal with you."

Cory's eyes widened in fear. "Hey, I said I was sorry."

"Oh, no!" Raven said. "I'm not about to hurt you, Cory." As she strode toward her brother, a huge grin lit up her face. "I'm going to give you a kiss for stepping up for me!"

Cory shuddered. He hated smooches, *especially* from his big sister. "No, Raven, no!" he cried, backing away in horror. "No!"

Raven suddenly stopped in her tracks. "Hey," she cried, seeing Cory backing away from her as if she were a horrible beast. "*That* was my vision!"

With a laugh, Raven started up again. Closer and closer she came until—

"Raven, no!" Cory cried.

But it was too late. The little man's fate was sealed with a kiss!

After Mr. and Mrs. Baxter got home from their trip, Cory and Raven were given new names—*Mr. and Ms. Clean!*

"Dad, come on, it's been two weeks," Raven complained. She stood at the kitchen sink, washing yet another pile of dirty dishes. "My hands are gonna be permanently pruny."

Mr. Baxter glanced up from his newspaper. "Both of you knew that a party was wrong," he said, "so you'll be doing these extra chores for a long, long time."

Cory stood next to Raven with a dish towel in his hand. Raven just washed the dishes. He was stuck drying them and putting them all away. "Are you ever going to leave us alone again?" he asked his dad.

"Maybe, when you're thirty," Mr. Baxter replied. "Besides, now your mom's got a new gadget. I don't know when I'll ever get her out of the house."

Mr. Baxter rose from his chair and walked to the kitchen door. Opening it, he peeked in on his wife.

"Yeeeehaa!" she cried from the living room. "Ride 'em, cowgirl!"

At the sink, Raven shook her head. *All right*, she thought, having the party without permission was not a great idea. But letting my mom try out that mechanical bull was probably the *stupidest* thing I've ever done!

Part Two

Chapter One

Ahhhh-chooo! Raven sneezed, sniffled, and wiped her sore nose. Yuck, she thought, another day with a miserable cold!

Yesterday, she'd missed school. But this morning, she'd dragged herself in for classes. Through bleary eyes, she peered down Bayside's crowded main hall and saw Eddie and Chelsea hanging at their lockers.

"Hey, what's up?" she asked, trudging over to them.

"Oh, hey, Rae," Chelsea said with a sympathetic smile. "How's that cold coming?"

Raven stifled another sneeze and forced a little smile. "I'm . . . I'm feeling a little better," she replied.

Eddie took one look at Raven and shuddered. His best friend might be "feeling" better, but she sure didn't look it. Her hair was stringy. Her clothes were wrinkled, and she clutched a box of tissues in one hand.

Then Raven blew her nose. The noise reminded Eddie of a foghorn on a misty night in San Francisco Bay—only much louder.

"Well, Rae," Eddie said, backing away, "at least you *look* good."

Raven nodded at Eddie's sweet comment. But as she turned from him, she heard him add something that wasn't so sweet—

Man, that hair is tore up.

Raven's head jerked toward Eddie in surprise. "What did you say about my hair?" she asked.

Eddie froze. "Um, nothing," he murmured in a sheepish voice. Then Raven heard him add, *Did I say that out loud?* This time, when

Eddie "spoke," she was looking right at him. And his mouth never moved!

Either my boy is learning ventriloquism, Raven thought, or something truly freakish is going down!

"Eddie, you didn't say that out loud," Raven told him. "But I think I heard it, like inside my head or something."

"What?" Chelsea's eyes widened as if Raven had said the coolest thing ever. "Rae, did you just read his mind?!"

Raven shrugged. "I don't know. Something weird is going on."

"Rae, ooh do me! Read my mind. Please, please," Chelsea begged. She sidled close to Raven and shut her eyes to concentrate.

Raven shrugged and stared at Chelsea. Intensely, she focused her psychic powers until she heard exactly what was going on in the girl's brain.

The sound of air filled Raven's head.

Dang, Raven thought. It's official. There is no intelligent life on Planet Chelsea.

"I'm not getting anything," Raven confessed to her best girlfriend. Okay, she added to herself, maybe I hear the faintest sound of crickets chirping, but not much else.

"Sorry, Chels."

But Chelsea wasn't worried. She smiled and clapped her hands. To her, this *proved* that Raven wasn't playing! "Wow, you *are* amazing," she gushed.

Raven sneezed again and groaned. "You know, I'm not sure what's going on. I've just got to go home and get to bed."

Just then, Suzette walked by. The cute foreign exchange student was in two of Raven's classes. As Eddie checked the girl out, his thoughts suddenly raced through Raven's mind.

"Eddie!" Raven cried in outrage.

"What?" Eddie said.

"You *know* what," Raven scolded, slapping his arm. "I heard that, ya nasty."

Then Raven grabbed Suzette's hand and pulled the girl down the hall, far away from Eddie—and his nasty thoughts!

Chapter Two

Raven left school early. It wasn't the sneezing and sniffling that sent her home. It was the constant mind reading!

During classes, kids' voices were saying all kinds of crazy things in her head. Raven did her best to ignore them. But then she heard what was actually going on in her teachers' minds, and she really started buggin'.

When she finally made it home, Raven found her mother sitting at the kitchen counter, leafing through a magazine.

Uh-huh! Denzel is looking fine!

It took Raven a moment to realize her mother was ogling a photo of hottie actor Denzel Washington. Raven shuddered. Here we go again, she thought, just like the teachers at school! Too much information!

"Mom, please stop what you're thinking." Because it is way embarrassing! Raven thought.

Mrs. Baxter suddenly closed the magazine. "Honey, I'm just reading my horoscope," she lied.

"And Denzel is *not* in your future," Raven told her sternly.

"What?" Mrs. Baxter said. She dropped the magazine and faced her daughter. "Okay, you're scaring me. What's going on?"

Raven rubbed her nose with a tissue. "Oh, nothing, it's this cold," she said. "I think there's some weird side effects or something."

Just then, Raven's father charged into the room. "Guess what?" he cried. "My mother is coming to stay with us this weekend."

Raven's face brightened. "Nana's coming?"

"Oh, honey, that's wonderful," Raven's mother told her father. But then Raven heard what her mom really thought: *Just what I need, an unexpected visit from that stuffy, old busybody!*

Unnerved by the reality check, Raven choked and started to cough. She'd never suspected that her mother didn't like Nana!

Mr. Baxter turned to his daughter. "Rae, is that cold still bothering you?" he asked with concern.

"Not as much as some *other* things," she muttered.

Mr. Baxter sat down at the kitchen counter next to his wife. "So, Tanya, are you okay with Mother staying with us?" he asked.

Suddenly, Raven heard him think, *She always says "fine," but she never means it.*

"Fine," Mrs. Baxter replied, then thought, *I always say "fine," but I never mean it.*

Raven's dad turned to her. "Oh, and Rae, remember, when Nana gets here, no talk about being psychic."

Mrs. Baxter frowned and touched her husband's hand. "Honey," she said, "maybe it's time we told your mother about Raven."

"No way!" Mr. Baxter replied. "You know how she reacted when we told her that *your* mom was psychic."

"It's true, she did have some issues," Mrs. Baxter said. Then she silently added, *She thought my mom was some kind of freaky "wooo-wooo"!*

Raven grimaced. *Dang,* she thought, this parental pot is about to boil over! "Look, look," she said quickly, "I hardly ever see Nana, and I love her so much. I wouldn't want to do anything to hurt her."

Mr. Baxter fumed. *At least somebody cares about my mother*, he thought.

Mrs. Baxter's eyebrows rose, and once again, Raven heard her thoughts: *At least somebody cares about his mother.*

Raven wanted to plug her ears, but she knew it wouldn't help. If only there was a way to plug my brain! she thought.

Raven sighed. She began to pace back and forth. Chewing her thumbnail, she realized, I can't tell them I'm reading their minds. They'll think I'm spying on them! Suddenly, she frowned. *Oh, snap,* she thought, I just read my own mind. . . . Oh, wait, everybody can do that!

Raven began to laugh—a little too hard.

Mr. Baxter eyed his daughter. "You okay, baby?" he asked.

Raven whirled and faced her parents. "Mom, Dad," she began. "I don't know how, but I can read your minds."

Strangely, Raven's mother didn't act

surprised at all. She just smiled knowingly, stood up, and gave Raven a big hug. "Honey," she said, "watery eyes, runny nose, reading minds . . . you have a psychic cold! My mother used to get them all the time. It only lasts a few days. You're going to be fine."

Raven was super-relieved.

But her father was not.

"Yeah, fine," he told Raven. "Now, *what* did you hear us thinking?"

Raven gulped and looked away. "I heard enough," she muttered.

Mr. and Mrs. Baxter exchanged guilty looks. And Raven hurried upstairs to her attic room, where she planned to hide for the rest of the evening!

The next morning, the Baxters' doorbell rang promptly at nine o'clock. Raven, Cory, and Mr. and Mrs. Baxter were all lined up in the foyer, dressed in their best clothes.

"Okay," Mr. Baxter said, adjusting his tie. "Mother's here. Just be yourselves."

Cory, standing stiffly in a dress shirt and tie, lost the smile he had pasted across his face. "Dad, if I was going to be *myself,* I'd be upstairs playing video games in my underwear!"

"Just behave," Mr. Baxter warned.

Then, Mr. Baxter took a deep breath and opened the front door. "Mother!" he cried and hugged the elegantly dressed woman.

Grandma Baxter's shoulder-length hair was iron gray but styled in a perfectly sleek flip. She wore smart glasses and a tailored suit. Raven always thought Nana Baxter was quite a sophisticated lady.

Opening her arms, Nana warmly hugged Raven's father. "My baby!" she cried. Then she opened her arms again to embrace Raven and Cory. "And my grandbabies!"

Finally, Nana Baxter faced Raven's mother. "And Tanya," she said flatly, her arms at her sides.

The two women stood staring uneasily at each other. Finally, they air kissed—with about two feet of space between them.

"Raven, how are you feeling, sweetheart?" Nana Baxter asked. "I hear you have a cold."

Raven was about to answer when she heard her grandmother silently snipe, *No wonder! Tanya does keep a drafty house.*

Raven squeezed her eyes shut. My cold must not be over yet, she realized, I just read Nana's mind!

"Actually, Nana, I'm feeling much better," Raven told her grandmother. "My mom just keeps it so *nice* and *toasty* in the house."

"Oh, well," Nana Baxter said, then went to her luggage and pulled out a long gift-wrapped box. "Cory, this is for you, sweetheart."

Cory took the gift, ripped the wrapping open, and gaped at the contents in happy surprise.

"It's a fishing rod," Nana said. "Your grandfather loved to fish."

Cory checked out the rod and grinned. "Man, this thing is off the heezee!"

Mr. Baxter sternly cleared his throat. "*Cory—*"

"I mean, thank you *ever* so much," the little boy quickly recited in a voice so polite even Miss Manners would have approved.

Nana Baxter smiled her own approval, then sat on the couch next to her granddaughter. "And I have a special surprise for you, Raven."

"Oh, Nana, you didn't have to get me anything," Raven replied.

"I didn't," Nana Baxter said.

Raven's face fell. And Cory's singsong thoughts broke into her head. *Raven got nothin'. Nana likes me better!*

Raven smirked.

"I'm saving your surprise for later," Nana explained.

"Ha!" Raven barked in Cory's ear.

Cory eyed his sister warily. Then he stood up. "Nana, I've got a surprise for you, too. I'd like you to meet Lionel."

Mr. Baxter reared back in horror. "Cory!" he cried. "I don't really think that's a good idea." But before he could stop his son, Cory had pulled his brown-and-white pet rat out of his pocket. With a smile of pride, the little boy displayed the squirming rodent to his grandmother.

"Get it away! Get it away!" Nana Baxter howled.

Raven's mother rushed over. "Mother Baxter, it's okay. Lionel is Cory's *pet* rat."

"Uh-huh," said Raven's father, shooing Cory and Lionel up the stairs. "A rat who'll be going on a little vacation for a few days. Cory, let's go!"

Later that morning, Cory sat in the kitchen, cuddling his beloved rodent. Eddie and Chelsea stood watching.

"I don't know if Lionel's ready for this," fretted Cory. "He's never been away from home."

Eddie sighed in frustration at Cory's drama-queen act. "He's just staying at my crib for a couple days. *Man up*, Cory!"

Cory nodded, dried a tear. "You're right," he said. "I have to be strong. For Lionel."

As Eddie held Lionel's cage, Cory slipped him inside.

Chelsea smiled at the squirmy rodent. "I can't believe our little Lionel is going on his first sleepover. I remember when he was this big—" She held her fingers two inches apart. "His little arms were this big—" Chelsea put her fingers together even closer. "And those itty-bitty teensy-weensy teeth were—"

Eddie rolled his eyes. "Okay, Chelsea, he was *small*. We get it."

"Here you go, Lionel," said Cory. He placed two tiny suitcases inside the cage. "I hope I didn't overpack."

Suddenly, Cory turned away, to hide a new flow of tears. "I'm going to miss you, buddy!" Cory sobbed.

Chelsea hugged Cory. "There's no stronger love than a boy and his rat," she declared.

"Yeah," Eddie said with a shudder. "There's also no *stranger* love."

Chapter Three

"**R**aven, I need to talk to you," called Mrs. Baxter, coming down the back stairs.

"I know," said Raven at the kitchen counter. "I read your mind."

"Right," said Mrs. Baxter. She walked up to her daughter and lowered her voice. "So, uh, you probably heard me thinking some things about your nana—"

Raven nodded. Oh, yeah, she thought. Sure did!

"I just want you to know that your nana is a wonderful person who loves you a lot," Mrs. Baxter continued. "It's just that sometimes she can be a real—Mother Baxter!"

Raven turned to see that Nana Baxter had

just walked into the kitchen. Whoa, that was close, Raven thought. Good save, Mom!

Nana Baxter smiled. "Tanya, may I borrow my granddaughter for a moment, *s'il vous plait*?"

Forcing a smile, Mrs. Baxter nodded and thought, *Why don't you just say "please" like everyone else!* Then, Mrs. Baxter noticed Raven staring at her. *Raven, did you hear that?* Mrs. Baxter thought in a panic.

Raven nodded to her mom as Nana Baxter led her granddaughter to the living room. "It's time for your surprise," Nana announced.

Laid out on the coffee table was a tea service with cream, sugar, and lemon wedges. Next to the cups and saucers sat a multileveled serving tray stacked with pretty little sandwiches and delicious pastries.

"A tea party!" Raven squealed in delight. "Just like we used to do when I was a little girl."

"Well," Nana remarked as the two sat down on the couch, "now that you're a young lady, we're not playing. I nominated you for membership in my social club, the White Glove Society!"

"Oh, yeah, that *is* a surprise," Raven said, forcing a smile. Mainly because she wasn't expecting to get signed up for that for about fifty or sixty years!

Raven shook out a napkin and hung it from her neck. Then she reached for a delicate tea sandwich. She sniffed the small, crustless rectangle, smelled a delicious mixture of cream cheese and chives and shoved the entire piece into her mouth.

"Well, this is for the junior chapter," Nana Baxter explained. "The admissions committee is coming for tea tomorrow, and we need to practice our etiquette."

"Right, Nana," Raven replied, cheeks

bulging with the delicate sandwich. "Do you really think that I'm White Glove material?"

Nana Baxter laid her hand on Raven's shoulder. "Of course you are. You're a Baxter. And don't worry, tomorrow is just a formality. You're as good as in."

Raven was about to reply when she felt a bolt of psychic energy rip through her body. Then everything around her spun like mad, as time itself appeared to stand still. . . .

Through her eye
The vision runs
Flash of future
Here it comes—

Okay, so what am I going to see now? Oh, snap, it's only my own front door. How boring is that?

Wait! The door is opening. . . .

It's a stampede!

A herd of old ladies is charging out of my house like it's on fire. They're all elegantly dressed, too—with hats and pearls and . . . Oh, no! White gloves! It's the White Glove Society!

They're knocking over tables, furniture, and anything else in their way. Oops! There goes the tea service! And, man, those ladies sure can scream!

As Raven's vision faded away, she felt someone tugging her arm. She blinked and saw Nana Baxter frowning at her.

"Raven," she scolded, "it's very poor etiquette to stare blankly into space with your mouth full."

Raven gulped down her food. "I'm sorry, Nana, it must be the cold." Then she remembered her vision, and a knot formed in the pit of her stomach that had nothing to do with the cream cheese sandwich she'd gobbled.

"Um . . ." Raven added, "maybe tomorrow's not such a good time for the committee to come over." *Especially if they're going to run screaming from the house like they did in my vision!*

"Oh, nonsense," Nana replied. "I've gone to a lot of trouble to arrange this tea. It's going to be a lovely afternoon."

"Oh, yeah," Raven replied with a nervous smile, "it's going to be a *scream*."

The next morning, Raven refused to get out of bed. After waking up, she simply fluffed her pillows and began reading a stack of fashion magazines.

Around eleven o'clock, Raven heard her mother climbing the back stairs. When she reached Raven's bedroom, she stood and stared at her daughter.

Why aren't you getting ready for the tea party? Raven heard her mother's thoughts. She lowered her magazine and sighed. "Mom," she said, "just because I can read your mind doesn't mean you should stop talking."

Mrs. Baxter laughed. "I know, but it's kind of fun."

A moment later, Mr. Baxter entered the attic bedroom. "Rae, what are you doing in bed?" he asked.

Raven frowned. "Dad, can you *please* just tell Nana that my cold came back? 'Cause I don't want to go to this tea party."

"What? Why not?" Mr. Baxter demanded.

"Because, Dad, I had a vision that it's going to get ugly," Raven explained. "People were screaming and running, and it's not 'cause they didn't like the tea."

Mrs. Baxter turned to confront her husband. "Okay, Victor," she said in a firm voice, "maybe *now* is the time to tell your mom that Raven is psychic."

Raven sat up in bed. "Yeah, Dad," she agreed. "If we tell her now, we can avoid this whole disaster."

Just then, a new set of footsteps sounded on the staircase and Nana Baxter appeared at the bedroom door. "So, what are we all talking about?" she asked, spying the little gathering.

Raven and her mother both stared at Raven's dad. He swallowed nervously, then spoke to Nana.

"Well, Mom, the truth is—" Mr. Baxter paused. Suddenly, he chickened out. "The truth is, your guests are coming any minute, and I have to put some sugar on the lemon bars!"

Raven was about to speak when her father's thoughts echoed inside her mind. *Sorry, Rae, it's not the right time.*

As Raven's parents headed back downstairs, her grandmother walked over to her bed and sat down. "Raven, a lady never stays in bed past ten," she scolded.

"Sorry, Nana, but I think my cold came back," Raven lied.

Nana Baxter frowned for a moment. Then she gave Raven a small, sweet smile and put an arm around her. "Well, if you're really that ill," she said gently, "maybe you should skip the tea party."

Nana hugged Raven tightly, then got up and pulled the covers around her. That's when Raven heard what Nana Baxter was really thinking—

I'll never let Raven know how she broke my heart.

Raven felt terrible. She didn't want to hurt Nana. Her vision was so awful—all she wanted to do was protect her grandmother. But, obviously, Raven was letting her down instead.

I have to do the tea party for Nana, Raven decided. I'll just have to find a way to prevent the thing from ending in disaster!

"Nana," Raven called, throwing off her bedcovers, "I think I'm feeling better."

"Oh, wonderful!" Nana Baxter exclaimed. "It was probably just a case of the nerves."

Raven stood up, and Nana Baxter held her arms open. "Oh, Raven," she said with joy. "You don't know how much this means to me!"

"I think I do," said Raven, hugging her grandma tight. I just hope you don't regret it!

Chapter Four

It was almost teatime. Raven had been dressing for an hour. Finally, she appeared at the top of the stairs in an outfit her grandma had bought for her to wear.

The conservative pink skirt fell well below her knees. The matching pink jacket had old-lady lace at the collar. An oversized silk flower dangled from the lapel. And on her head was a hat with a brim so wide it hid half her face. She wore pearls around her neck, held a pink handbag, and balanced precariously on high-heeled pink pumps.

Dang, Raven thought, I don't want to hurt my grandma's feelings, but in this getup I feel like I've been *punked* with pink.

"Nana," Raven said as she wobbled down the steps, "do you really think this is a good ensemble? I mean, I don't really feel comfortable in this. It's just not right for me."

"Oh, nonsense," Nana Baxter replied, spinning her granddaughter to examine her outfit. "You look divine. The committee is going to love you."

Ding-dong!

Nana heard the doorbell and opened the door. Eight elderly women stood there. They were all elegantly attired in their Sunday best. Each wore a pair of spotless white gloves.

"Welcome, ladies. I'd like you to meet my darling granddaughter, Raven," Nana Baxter said with obvious pride.

"Wassup! How y'all doin'—" Raven started, then suddenly stopped. She'd never seen so many unhappy wrinkled faces.

Whoops, my bad, she thought, these ain't

homegirls. Time to switch to old-lady talk.

"Uh, I mean, charmed," Raven quickly corrected. Then she gave them her very best curtsy—and almost fell on her face. Man, these heels are whack!

Nana Baxter gestured to the large table set up in the middle of the living room. Displayed against a bright pink tablecloth was a feast of pastries, sandwiches, scones, and two steaming teapots.

"Why don't we all take our seats and have some tea," Nana Baxter said.

A large, imposing gray-haired woman named Miss Penelope made sure to sit right next to Raven. When they were all seated, Miss Penelope glanced up and imperiously commanded, "Mrs. Baxter, please lead us in the White Glove Society oath."

"Certainly," Nana replied. She stood up and cleared her throat. "I promise to always practice good manners, good grooming, and to uphold the standards of the White Glove Society."

When the ladies were finished, they crossed their wrists over their hearts. Then they made their hands flutter like butterfly wings.

Miss Penelope turned to smile at Raven. "You know, every time your grandmother comes to town, she never fails to tell us all about your *wonderful* accomplishments."

Raven returned Miss Penelope's friendly smile, until she heard the *thoughts* coming out of the woman's head. *The old windbag. My grandson's a brain surgeon, you don't hear me bragging.*

"Oh!" Raven said in shock. When everyone turned to look at her, she quickly added, "Uh, let's get this party started, then."

Because the sooner it starts, Raven added to herself, the sooner it will *end*!

* * *

Cory glumly sat at the kitchen table. All morning, he'd been looking at his Lionel scrapbook, *My Rat and Me*, and reliving his favorite moments with his furry friend.

As Raven's tea party started in the next room, the back door opened, and Eddie and Chelsea entered. Eddie was carrying Lionel's cage. Chelsea was holding the rat's tiny luggage.

"Cory," Eddie said, "this isn't really working out."

"Lionel, you're back!" Cory cried. He snatched the cage out of Eddie's hand and set it on the counter. Cory opened the door, reached in, and petted his beloved pal. Lionel looked very cute this morning. Someone had even dressed him in his little red sweater and a harness for his return.

"Hey, man, we had to bring him home,"

Eddie explained, dropping into a chair at the kitchen table. "There was just too much crying going on."

"Lionel was crying?" Cory asked worriedly. He stepped over to the kitchen table to hear more.

"No, I was," Eddie replied. "The little rascal kept me up all night. Squeak, squeak, squeak! Man, change the tune or something!"

"Yeah," said Chelsea. "It's weird, you know? To cheer him up, I put on his little leash to take him for a walk, but I don't know, Lionel was so depressed, it was kind of more like a drag."

Cory frowned. "Man, I knew he was too young to be away from home." He turned around to pet Lionel again. But when he approached the cage, which was sitting on the kitchen counter, he saw that the door had been left open. Lionel was gone!

"Lionel?" Cory cried. He called and called, but his pet rat was nowhere to be found.

In the Baxters' living room, the White Glove Society's tea party was well under way. Nana Baxter pointed to the beautifully presented table setting.

"So, hasn't Raven set a lovely table?" Nana asked her fellow club members.

"Divine," said Miss Penelope.

Raven was about to thank the woman until she heard her silently add, *Raven this, Raven that. Why doesn't Mrs. Baxter stuff a sock in it?*

Raven's jaw dropped in outrage. Listen up, old woman, I'll tell you where to stuff that sock! But Raven quickly caught herself. I can't say that. I can't say anything. My grandmother doesn't know I'm psychic, and I have to keep my mouth shut.

Covering her reaction, Raven flashed Miss Penelope a big, fake smile.

"So, Raven," Miss Penelope purred. "What are your future goals and ambitions?"

Every wrinkled face around the big table turned her way and stared expectantly.

Raven gulped, feeling the pressure. "Well, um," she nervously replied, "I'd really love to study fashion design and—" Suddenly, Raven spotted Cory's little furry rat scurrying across the mantel. "Lionel!" she exclaimed.

Raven jumped to her feet and raced to the mantel. But when she got there, Lionel had already moved on.

Miss Penelope frowned. "Did she say *vinyl*? I hope that's not coming back."

"Yes, ladies, so do I," Raven said, turning back to the tea party table. "I hope vinyl doesn't come back either, 'cause that was just ridiculous. Don't you think?"

Raven took her seat again. "But as I was saying, I would definitely love to study fashion design—"

Suddenly, the piano tinkled. Lionel was racing across the keys. Raven hopped to the piano and ran her fingers across the ivories to cover the rodent's little recital. "—and music. Music," she quickly cried. "Actually, ladies, I wrote something for tonight's festivities."

She stood over the piano and played a few notes. "It's something for the White Glove Society," Raven continued. "A song I like to call—"

Again Raven spied Lionel. This time he raced across the rug and disappeared under the tea table. Raven abandoned the piano and rushed back to the ladies.

"Oh, um, forget about that song," she said, "because it's not quite finished yet." To cover her crazy behavior, she lifted the silver cover on a serving plate. Beneath was a perfectly arranged offering of lemon bars.

"Why don't you guys enjoy the lemon bars that my dad made for tonight," she suggested, passing them around. "I'm sure you guys would love them. One calorie! Enjoy those lemon bars, ladies, 'cause they're so soft and lemony—"

As Raven babbled, she kept moving around the table, looking for any sign of Lionel. This time when his twitchy little whiskers showed themselves, she took no chances. She fell on her hands and knees, and trapped the rat beneath her wide-brimmed hat.

"Gotcha!" Raven cried in triumph.

Every member of the White Glove Society turned to face Raven. She was still on the rug, clutching the hat.

"Uh, I'm ch-checking out the f-floor," Raven stammered, rising to her feet. "Making sure it's sturdy for the hat dance."

Raven took a few bouncy dance steps around the hat, just to make her point. With each step, she moved the hat a little closer to the kitchen door.

"That was the entertainment for tonight," Raven said at last. "Now I'm just going to retire to, um, check on the fudge."

Nana Baxter rose, wringing her hands. Clearly, the woman was confused about Raven's strange behavior. "Raven, darling," she said tightly, "we didn't make any fudge."

"Wow!" said Raven, amazed. "Then I'd better get started. Are you sure we didn't make any?"

The ladies eyed Raven with suspicion. She could hear their thoughts, and they weren't pretty. But Raven didn't stop. With a bright pink pump, she pushed the hat all the way to the kitchen door.

Raven knew her grandmother was upset,

but Raven wasn't. She was *relieved.* All morning, that vision of the old women stampeding had been weighing on her.

But now that I've captured Cory's rat, Raven thought, I know I've mastered that disaster!

Chapter Five

"**L**ionel, come out, boy!" Cory called.

Cory had searched the kitchen from top to bottom, desperate to find his squeaky friend. Eddie and Chelsea were looking, too. They'd checked under the kitchen table and behind the sink. Chelsea even checked inside the refrigerator!

Then, Raven came through the kitchen door, still pushing her hat with her shoe. "I think I have what you're looking for," she declared.

Everyone gathered around the hat, ready to pounce on Lionel the second Raven freed him.

"Here we go. Here we go," Raven said, clutching the brim. But when she lifted the hat, there was no rat!

"*Oh, snap!* He's not there!" Raven cried in a panic. "He must still be out there with the ladies. If they see him, they're going to run and scream, just like in my vision."

The door opened again. Nana Baxter backed into the kitchen. "I'll return in a moment," she called to the other members of the White Glove Society. "Just carry on, ladies." Then she closed the door between the rooms and spun to face her granddaughter.

"Raven! Why are you acting like this?" she demanded in a stern voice.

"Nana, you have to believe me," Raven replied. "I'm trying to make a good impression. It's just that, uh, the people right here— my friends and Cory—they're having a crisis."

Nana Baxter glanced at Raven's friends. Eddie looked sheepish. Cory looked guilty. And Chelsea's expression was a complete blank.

Nana put her hands on her hips. "Are you telling me the truth?" she asked her granddaughter. "Because I smell a rat."

"Really?" cried Cory excitedly. "Which way did he go?"

Raven covered her brother's face with her party hat and shoved him backward. Then she hurried to her grandmother's side and began to usher her to the door.

"Nana, everything is under control, okay?" said Raven. "Just go out there, sit down, and tell the ladies to flutter. Flutter, flutter, flutter!"

When Nana was gone, Raven turned back to Cory, Eddie, and Chelsea. "I've got to get back to the tea party in there," Raven hissed. "And you guys have *got* to get that Lionel *out* of the living room—"

All three nodded obediently and immediately lunged for the door. But Raven leaped in front of them and blocked their path.

"—but," she warned them, "you can't go *in* the living room." Then, Raven straightened her pink jacket and prepared to return to the tea party. "Good luck," she whispered before closing the door in their faces.

Eddie threw up his hands. "What are we going to do?" he cried in exasperation.

Chelsea chewed her lower lip and tried to think of something.

But it was Cory who snapped his fingers. He knew exactly what to do. Looks like I'll be using Grandma's gift after all, he thought.

Upstairs in his room, Cory rolled back the rug to expose an air vent.

Chelsea was surprised to see the hole in the floor. Wow! she thought. I can see the whole living room through this vent. Those lemon bars sure look tasty!

While Chelsea checked out the tea party

action, Eddie watched Cory tie a small cube of cheddar cheese on the end of his new fishing rod.

"Okay," Cory said. "This vent goes down to the living room. I drop the cheese through the vent, Lionel finds it—he loves his cheese! We catch onto his harness, reel him up, problem solved!"

Eddie rubbed the back of his neck. "That's the dumbest plan ever."

But Chelsea nodded enthusiastically. "It just might work."

Carefully, Cory lowered the cheese through the vent.

Meanwhile, down in the living room, the tea party was still in full swing.

Miss Penelope rose and called for attention. "Raven, the ladies and I have an announcement. We are pleased to admit you as a junior member into the White Glove Society."

The other ladies put their white gloves together in gracious applause. But inside Raven's head, Miss Penelope's thoughts weren't so gracious. *I just hope she's not a blowhard like her grandmother*, Raven heard her think.

"Hey!" Raven cried, frowning at the old battle-ax.

"Raven!" Nana Baxter warned, seeing her granddaughter's angry expression.

Raven reattached her smile. "I mean . . . hooray! Hooray, everybody!"

The ladies applauded again, and Raven stood up. "Thank you so much. I accept. Wonderful tea party." Then she moved toward the door. "Drive safe. Buh-bye!"

But Miss Penelope wagged her finger. "Not so fast, Raven. I still have the honor of presenting you with your first pair of white gloves."

Raven tried to look impressed. "Oh, wow."

Miss Penelope picked up her purse, which had been sitting on the floor. She pulled a small square box out of it. But when she lifted the lid, only one glove was inside.

"How odd," Miss Penelope said. "I specifically packed two gloves."

Raven glanced at the floor in time to see a white glove scurrying across the rug on little rat legs. *Lionel!*

"Oh, you know what?" said Raven tensely. "They don't always travel in pairs."

Then Raven noticed something dangling near her head—a piece of cheese at the end of a fishing line.

"Cheese?" Raven gasped in surprise.

"Cheese? Who said cheese?" the ladies asked.

"Uh, I mean, *say* cheese, for the camera!" Raven cried. "That's it, everybody, cheese. I just want to take a picture to remember this lovely moment. Please, everyone over here."

Raven coaxed the White Glove Society members to their feet. Quickly, she turned the ladies away from the dangling cheddar.

"Oh, fabulous!" she gushed. "Let's all go over here by the fireplace. Perfect! Flutter, flutter, flutter! Ladies, stay right there, and let me get the camera."

Raven circled behind the women and gazed up at the ceiling. Through the vent, she saw Cory dangling his fishing rod.

Up in Cory's bedroom, Eddie was growing impatient. "Any luck?" he asked.

Cory shrugged. "They're just not biting today."

Beside Cory and Eddie, Chelsea sat back and smiled at the fishing rod. "Yeah, but sometimes it's just nice to get away from it all."

Cory smacked his forehead. If that girl's

cranium gets any lighter, her head is gonna float away, he thought.

Downstairs, the cheese had finally reached the floor. The elderly ladies hadn't noticed. They were posing for Raven, their gloved hands still fluttering.

"Um, ladies, don't move," Raven said, still searching for a camera. "Everyone just stay where you are—"

Raven watched that single white glove scurry across the rug toward the waiting cheese. After a few tentative sniffs, the rat beneath the glove took a big bite.

"Seriously, don't move," Raven warned the women.

Upstairs, Cory exploded with excitement. "I've got something!"

"Reel it in," Eddie yelled.

As Lionel chewed the cheese, the fishing hook caught his harness, just as Cory had predicted. Slowly, Cory reeled his rat off the floor. The little rodent rose up, up, up, toward the ceiling.

In the living room, Raven's horrified eyes followed the sight. She glanced at the White Glove Society ladies. Luckily, they were still babbling and fluttering amongst themselves, completely oblivious to Cory's raising of the rat behind their backs.

Then something terrible happened. The rat elevator stopped dead.

"Uh-oh," Cory said up in his bedroom. "The reel got jammed."

Up! Up! Get that rat out of here, Cory! Raven screamed inside her head. She wished she could send out brain signals as well as she received them!

The rat was now dangling at eye level, mere inches from the ladies' backs. His tiny feet wiggled. His little nose sniffed the air.

And, at that very moment, Nana Baxter turned around.

Chapter Six

Impatient with waiting for Raven to snap her picture, Nana called out, "Raven, what are you—" Suddenly, she found herself staring directly into a pair of beady little rodent eyes.

Nana screamed. The other ladies turned to see what was wrong. Then, everyone was screaming!

"Flying rats!" Miss Penelope yelled. "Flee, ladies! Flee!"

The dignified members of the White Glove Society were now racing around like nutcases, arms waving.

One lady jumped up on a chair, fearing a herd of rats might be swarming the floor. But she lost her footing and crashed into the middle of the big round table. Cups, saucers, and cakes went flying.

Raven cringed. Well, there goes the tea service, she thought, with that old familiar feeling of déjà vu.

Cory, Chelsea, and Eddie heard the screams of terror in the living room below. Eddie peeked through the vent. "Man, some of those ladies can *move*," he said, impressed.

At last, Cory got the fishing reel to work again. "Hey, it's loose!" he cried. He started turning again and Lionel started rising.

"Come to Papa!" Cory cried with joy when Lionel finally made it up to the bedroom. He grabbed his pet and gently hugged him. "Welcome home, buddy."

The world below might have been in total chaos. But above it all, Cory couldn't have been happier.

"Ladies! Ladies!" Raven shouted. "He's not really flying! He's just a pet rat!"

Raven tried her best, but no one was paying attention. She doubted the women could even hear her through their hysterical screams.

Surrendering, Raven threw up her hands, dropped onto the couch, and cried, "Oh, go ahead. *Flee!*"

Raven's parents were just striding up the front walkway. They had left the house earlier to give Raven and her grandmother some privacy with their tea party. While they were out, Raven's mother had a long talk with her husband. She'd finally convinced him that it was time for Nana to know the truth about her granddaughter.

"Yeah, you're right, Tanya," Mr. Baxter told his wife as they approached the front door. "I need to stand up to my mother once and for all."

"Thank you," Mrs. Baxter said.

Then Raven's father opened the door—and saw a stampede of screaming society ladies coming at him like a tidal wave.

Mrs. Baxter leaped clear, but Mr. Baxter wasn't so lucky. The women washed over him, knocking the big man to the front-porch floor.

When the ladies were gone, he stumbled to his feet. "Okay," he said, "that hurt."

Together, Raven's parents rushed into the living room. They couldn't believe their eyes. The living room was a total wreck.

Nana Baxter stood in the center of it all, a look of misery on her face.

"This is a disaster," Nana Baxter said with a sad sigh. She sat down in one of the only chairs still upright.

"Raven, why did you behave like this?" Nana Baxter asked.

Raven stepped forward, head down. "Nana," she said in a soft voice, "there's something I wish I could tell you."

Raven looked at her father. To her surprise, Mr. Baxter nodded his agreement. Raven pulled up an overturned chair and sat down next to her grandmother.

"Nana, I'm psychic," Raven proclaimed.

Nana Baxter waved her words aside. "Oh, that's preposterous," she said.

But Raven shook her head. "No, it's . . . uh, *posterous*. I mean, I had a vision that this tea party was going to be a disaster."

Nana Baxter was silent. But Raven heard her thoughts: *Oh, no. Another "wooo-wooo" in the family.*

"Nana, I'm not a 'wooo-wooo.' I'm your granddaughter," Raven proudly replied.

Nana Baxter's face registered shock. "How did you know that I—"

"Oh, yeah," Raven explained. "I also have a psychic cold, so I can temporarily read minds."

Nana frowned at her granddaughter, looking hurt. "And you kept this from me all these years?"

Before Raven could say a word, Mr. Baxter quickly stepped up. "Mother, it's my fault," he said. "Raven and Tanya wanted to tell you, but I didn't think you'd accept it."

"Why would you think that?" Nana asked.

"Because Tanya's mother is psychic and you didn't accept her," Mr. Baxter replied.

"That's not true," Nana argued.

Mr. Baxter crossed his arms and lifted an eyebrow. "*Mother . . .*"

Nana sniffed. "Maybe it's a *little* true," she admitted.

"Now, *Mother . . .*" Mr. Baxter pressed.

"Don't push it, Victor," Nana snapped. Then, to everyone's surprise, she turned to Raven's mother and *apologized*. "Tanya, I'm sorry," she said. "I really did judge your mother without knowing her. And if she's anything like Raven, I made a terrible mistake. You must think I'm awful."

Raven hurried to her grandmother's side. "Never, Nana," she said. "It's okay, we love you. You're Nana."

Raven gave her grandma a big hug.

"We're family," Mrs. Baxter agreed.

With a relieved smile, Nana opened her arms to Mrs. Baxter. And this time she hugged her just as warmly as Raven.

"Oh, and one more thing," Raven said when the hugs were done. "You might need to watch your back with that Miss Penelope. 'Cause she ain't playin' with you."

Nana Baxter nodded knowingly. "I always

suspected that. Well, you know, I think I'm through with her and the White Glove Society." Then she slapped her knee and laughed. "Although this last meeting was off the heezee!"

Raven clapped her hands in delight. "Oh, yeah! Hit it, Nana! Bring it down!"

Later that afternoon, Mr. Baxter went looking for his son. He found him in his bedroom, holding his fishing rod and reeling something up through the floor vent.

"Cory, I told you it's dangerous to pull Lionel through that vent," Mr. Baxter scolded.

"I know," Cory replied as he finished jerking the fishing line upward. Dangling from its end was a square of pastry dusted with powdered sugar. "But you didn't say anything about lemon bars!"

Cory pulled the lemon bar free. "Baby, baby!" he whooped. "Wanna bite?"

Mr. Baxter sat down next to his son. "Okay, little man. Let's share."

As Cory passed his dad the dessert, they heard Nana, Mrs. Baxter, and Raven through the floor vent. The three were talking and laughing together in the living room.

Life is sweet, Mr. Baxter decided as he licked powdered sugar off his fingers. *And so are my lemon bars!*

Gaze into the future and take a sneak peek at the next *That's So Raven* story. . . .

Queen of Hearts

Adapted by Jasmine Jones

Based on the television series, "That's So Raven", created by Michael Poryes and Susan Sherman

Based on the episode written by Sarah Jane Cunningham & Suzie V. Freeman

Ooh, someone must have been doing some decorating around here, Raven Baxter thought as she walked out of her English classroom and into the hallway at Bayside High School. Because that locker is looking *good*. She stopped in her tracks, a grin curling at the corners of her mouth. She particularly liked the way they'd added a tall, dark, and gorgeous guy standing right in front of it.

While his back was still turned toward her, Raven hurried over to the guy and placed her hands over his eyes. "Guess who?" she cooed. "She's sweet, adorable . . ." Raven cocked an eyebrow. ". . . and she's gonna get real mad if you get it wrong."

"Hey, Rae," Devon said, turning to face her.

Give that boy two points for correct guessing under pressure, Raven thought as she pulled away her hands. Of course, given that I call him after every class period, it's probably not too challenging to recognize my voice.

"Hey, you win a kiss . . ." Raven said brightly. She puckered up and leaned in for a little smooch. Mmmm, she thought as her heart fluttered in her chest. De-licious. "Thank you very much." She smiled and pressed her hands together eagerly. "So, you wanna hang out tonight?"

Devon thought for a moment. "Um," he hedged, "tonight's not really good." He turned back to face his locker, and Raven was left looking at his black backpack.

For a minute, Raven wasn't sure what to say. Tonight's not good? she thought. I think he must mean, it's not good if we're *not* hanging out, right? Should I ask him to clarify?

Turning back to face Raven, Devon gave her an apologetic smile.

Okay, he means tonight's not good, period, she realized. But I'm not going to freak out and get all clingy-girlfriend on him. Guys need space. Raven had read that in a magazine. Hunter time, it was called. Time to stare into the fire and think about . . . beasts. Or something. Anyway, guys needed it, and if Devon needed some hunter time, he was going to get it. "Okay," Raven said brightly. "I'm not gonna pry. You know, I'm not gonna be one of those girlfriends who's all up in your business."

Devon's face relaxed into a grin. "Oh, cool," he said warmly, his dark eyes glowing. "Thanks, Rae." He patted her on the shoulder and started to walk away.

"Bye!" Raven called sweetly as she watched his red shirt retreat down the hall. "Bye, Devon! Bye, sweetie. I'll talk to you later, okay?"

Devon gave her a little wave.

"Somethin' is definitely going on with that boy," Raven announced, as her best friends, Chelsea Daniels and Eddie Thomas, walked over to join her. Raven narrowed her eyes. *And I do not like it when something is going on with Devon . . . besides me.*

Chelsea lifted her eyebrows. "You and Devon okay?"

"Oh, yeah, I'm fine." Raven cast a suspicious glance down the hallway, where Devon's back had just disappeared behind some double doors. "It's just he's been acting weird all week." She turned to her best guy friend. "Eddie, you're a guy, what do you think's going on?"

Eddie heaved a thoughtful sigh as he fidgeted with the strap on his black messenger bag. "Well, normally, Rae, when a guy acts like that, it means he's got something big on his mind," he said. "Or something small." He shrugged. "Or maybe he's just hungry."

Why do I ever ask Eddie's advice on relationships? Raven wondered as she gave her best guy friend a heavy-lidded glare. The boy is no Dr. Phil. "Why do you answer when you really don't even know?"

Eddie shook his head and grinned. "I'm a guy. It's what we do." With a little wave, he strutted off down the hall. "Holla."

Through her eye
The vision runs
Flash of future
Here it comes—

What's this? Devon and Chelsea, all cozy together by the lockers? Since when do those two tell each other secrets?

"Check this out."

Oooh, is Devon holding out what I think he's holding out? Okay, that's a little black velvet box. And there's only one thing that comes in a little black velvet box. . . .

Okay, I've known my girl Chelsea for a long time—but I've never seen her eyes bug out like that. Better tell her that it's not a good look.

"Oh, my goodness! Devon, this is beautiful. Raven's gonna love it!"

Oh, snap! A gift—for me?

And don't I always say that the best gifts come in teeny-tiny black boxes?

In the next moment, Raven was back in the present, looking into Chelsea's face. Raven put her hands over her eyes. "Chels!" she screeched. "I know why Devon has been acting weird. He bought me jewelry!" Her hands fluttered in front of her face, flapping in excitement.

"What?" Chelsea gave her a quit-playing look.

Oh, there she goes with that eyes-bugging-out thing, Raven thought. But she didn't have time to warn her friend—she was too excited about Devon!

Raven tossed her long, jet-black hair. "And Chelsea," she said breathlessly, "you're the one who saw it and you said—"

Chelsea's hand went to her chest. "What?"

" 'Oh, my goodness,'" Raven finished, " 'Raven's gonna love it.'"

"I did?" Chelsea shook her head and smiled proudly. "Raven, I love when I'm in your visions. It's like, it's like I'm starring in my own little movie that only you can see."

"That's adorable," Raven said sweetly. Then her tone turned serious. "Now listen up." She grabbed Chelsea's arm and pulled her in for a conference. "I want you to follow Devon, okay? Because you're the only one who knows what he got me." She squeezed her best friend's hand. I'm counting on you, Chelsea, she thought.

Chelsea seemed to get it. She nodded, her face serious. "Okay."

Time to put on some pressure. Raven wrapped her arm around Chelsea's shoulders. "As the star of my vision, I'm trusting you to make this one come true," Raven went on, gesturing grandly.

Chelsea bit her lip. "Right. Okay." She didn't move.

And why is the star of my vision still stand-ing here in front of me? Raven wondered. "Well, what are you waiting for? Go on into the future with yourself!"

Chelsea rolled her eyes. "Well, Rae," she said in her hel-lo-what-do-you-*think*-I'm-wait-ing-for? voice. "You didn't say 'action.'"

Oh, there's going to be some action if this girl doesn't get going, Raven thought. But she was not about to upset the star of her most exciting vision ever. Without Chelsea, the vision wouldn't come true. And Raven wouldn't let that happen.